Frieda B.™
and the Finkledee Ink

by Renata Bowers

pictures by Michael Chesworth

I dedicate this book to those in my life who believed in my gift of writing before I did.
My deepest thanks to each of you for extending a yellow pencil to me:

* My first grade teacher, Jean Dorn

* My high school language arts teacher, Professor Moldenhauer

* My first boss — who took a risk in hiring me — Don Carlsen

* My second boss — who took a risk in hiring me — Helen Vollmer

Other titles in the Frieda B. series:

Frieda B. Herself

Frieda B. Meets the Man in the Moon

Frieda B. and the Zillabeast

Copyright © 2014 by Renata Bowers
All rights reserved.

ISBN #978-0-9843862-2-2.

First Edition.
Library of Congress Control Number: 2014912669
Printed in the United States.

To visit Frieda and/or order additional
books from the Frieda B. series, go to
www.FriedaB.com.

Ink is ink, don't you think?
Isn't all ink the same?

One would think.
But one ink with an odd-sounding name
promised more – so much more, that our friend Frieda B.
spent her every last cent just to try it and see.

It all started one day up in Fiddle-Dee-Dee.
A young man came to town; so peculiar was he
that he soon drew a crowd of a hundred or more,
each one craning and straining to see what he wore.

For his clothes were uncommon, from shoulders to shoes —
busy circles and stripes in a rainbow of hues.
Oh, but more than his clothes were the words that he spoke.
For he promised great things to those Fiddle-Dee folk.

"Come and see!" the man bellowed. "And soon you will think there is nothing on earth quite like Finkledee Ink! It's pure magic, I say! And for those of you who dream of writing great stories, then this ink's for you!

Because Finkledee Ink nearly writes by itself –
stories better than those on your library shelf.
Just a penful of ink will soon make you a master.
To be a great author, why there's nothing faster.

It may cost a bit more than you'd usually spend,
but can one put a price tag on dreams, my dear friends?
I'll be here just today, then be gone in a blink.

So don't miss
      your one
            chance
                  to own..."

At the front of the crowd, Frieda B. stared in awe
as she heard what she heard and she saw what she saw.
For it stirred a deep longing she held in her heart
to become a great writer. This ink *was her start!*

She and Zilla raced home, for they hadn't much time.
Frieda emptied her bank of each quarter and dime.
Then she counted each coin with a soft little clink…
There was just enough money, for one jar of ink.

To the center of town Frieda took every cent,
to the brightly-clothed man in his ink-selling tent.

He took all of her coins with a smile and a wink,
in return for one jar full of Finkledee Ink.

The glass, it was shiny. The ink was deep blue.
Just what secrets this jar of ink held, no one knew.
Oh, but Frieda was certain as certain could be
that inside of this jar was the start of a dream.

A *big* dream… so important, so deep in her heart,
Frieda took every step to ensure a good start:

She chose books that she loved, to provide inspiration.
She filled up her walls with great words and quotations.
She listened to songs – let them sink, sink, sink in…
Then with head and heart full, she was set to begin.

Frieda picked up her pen, filled with Finkledee Ink,
and she wove the best tale that her thinker could think.
It was marvelous, really – a story so grand
Frieda hardly believed that it came from her hand.

The next day, Frieda B. brought her story to school.
Upon reading, her teacher exclaimed, "It's a jewel!"
"Frieda B.," declared she, "oh you must write some more!
I can only imagine what else lies in store.

What you have is a gift – yes, a great gift indeed
to a world that is hungry for good things to read."

Just as water and sunshine make tiny seeds grow,
the belief of her teacher made Frieda's heart glow.
"I'm a writer!" she mused. "A great teller of tales!
And with Finkledee Ink in my pen, I can't fail."

So with pen in her hand and great faith in her heart,
Frieda B. a whole series of stories did start.

There was one of a girl who
would only eat butter.

A golfer who played
all nine holes with one putter.

A cat who baked crackers to feed to the fish.

And a young man who never gave up on his wish.

Frieda wrote one such gripping and nail-biting caper,
it made the front page of the Fiddle-Dee paper.

She wrote and she wrote with her heart full of glee,
'til with one sudden stroke and the cross of a "T"…

...Frieda's one jar of ink off her table did soar!

Then it shattered. And splattered, all over her floor,
'til the last drop of Finkledee Ink… was no more.

Frieda B. stared in silence, unable to think,
for her heart was as shattered as that jar of ink.

"It's all over," she thought, "as a writer, I'm through.
Without Finkledee Ink, there's no dream to pursue.

It's because of that ink that my teacher was awed.
And now all will find out: I'm a phony – a fraud."

As she brooded her doom, little Zilla came near
with a new yellow pencil behind his left ear.
And with eyes and a heart full of love for his friend,
Zilla nudged her to take it, to write once again.

And although Frieda B. didn't feel it inside,
the belief of her friend gave her courage to try.
She sat down at her desk, with that pencil in hand,
and...

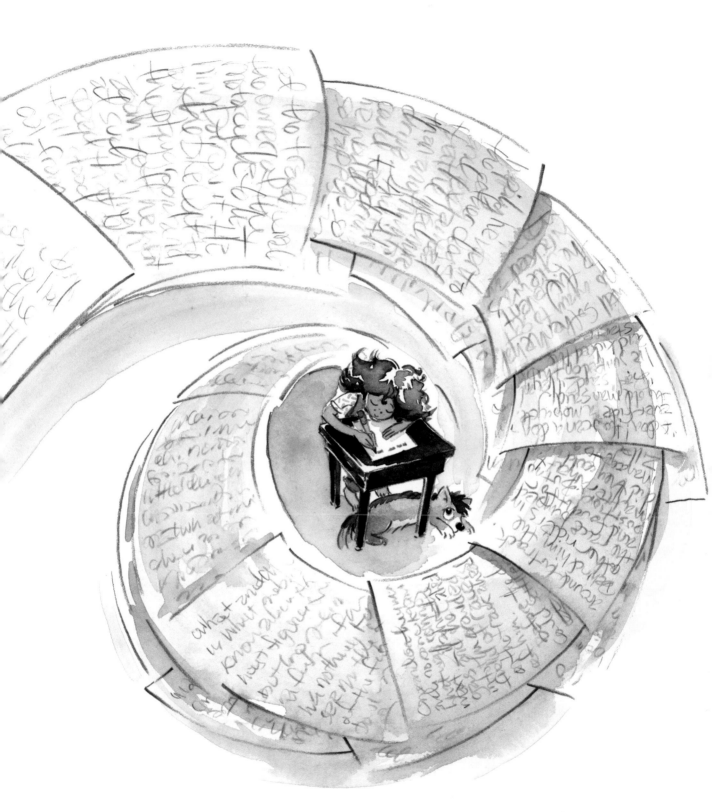

…began weaving a tale that was grander than grand.

There was no need for ink – in fact, pencil was best!
And with Zilla beside her, she wrote with great zest –
a grand tale full of dreams and one very good friend.
A tale that was perfect, beginning to end.

Frieda finished that story with great peals of laughter...

...And from that day on, she wrote
happily
ever
after.